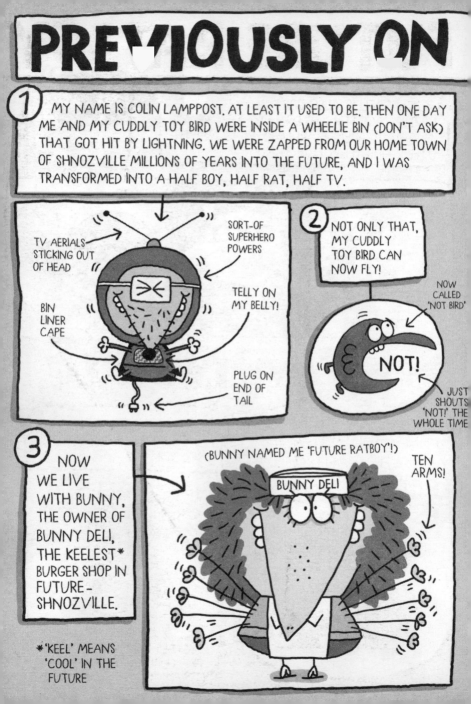

# CHEESE-BLEURGHER "MEAL" DEAL

Probably the best thing about getting zapped millions of years into the future and turned into a superhero rat is that I don't have to go to school any more. (Kids don't go to school in the future.)

HOVER-CAR PARK

SHNOZVILLE ~~SCHOOL~~

'What've you got planned for today, kiddywinkles?' said Bunny one mornkeels, peering out the window at Shnozville High Street.

I was sitting in Bunny Deli with my best friends Twoface, Jamjar and Splorg. Oh yeah, and my sidekick Not Bird too.

'Oh not much, probably just gonna hang around here eating cheesebleurghers,' said Splorg.

A cheesebleurgher is a cheeseburger that goes 'BLEURGH!' when you bite into it, by the way.

'Good idea, Splorgy Baby!' said Twoface, his two faces grinning. 'Four Cheesebleurgher Meal Deals for me and my pals please, Malcolm!' he shouted.

'Coming right up!' said Malcolm, the official Bunny Deli Smellnu, and four Cheesebleurgher Meal Deals fizzled to life in front of our eyes.

MALCOLM

A Smellnu is a floating menu, invented by Jamjar. It lets you smell the things that're on it, in case you didn't know.

Oh yeah, and a Cheesebleurgher Meal Deal is a cheesebleurgher, a packet of zigzaggedy-shaped chips and a cup of whatever drink you were thinking of at the exact billisecond the meal fizzled to life.

Jamjar sniffed her drink.

SNIFF

BUNNY DELI

'YUCK, Hedgehog Cola! Why do I ALWAYS think of Hedgehog Cola?' she said, throwing her cup towards Dennis, the official Bunny Deli bin.

'Ooh, I'll have that!' said Bunny, shooting one of her ten arms out and catching the Hedgehog Cola before it landed in Dennis.

'Couldn't do me a favour could you, gang?' she said, sipping on the drink, and we all nodded but didn't say anything, because our mouths were full of cheesebleurghers.

'Here's a list with a few bits I need from the shops,' she smiled, and a glowing yellow square with scribbly writing on it floated up from the counter and hovered next to her face.

'Ah, glad to see you're using my latest invention, Bunny!' smiled Jamjar. 'The Floaty Note 6000!'

'Ooh, it's ever so useful!' said Bunny, patting Jamjar on the head.

The shopping list wafted over to Twoface's two faces, and he squinted his four eyes, trying to read what was on it.

# WHAT WAS WRITTEN ON THE FLOATY NOTE:

'What kind of boring old shopping list is that?' said Twoface.

Bunny held all her fingers up and gave them a waggle. 'You'd be surprised how quickly that stuff runs out when you've got ten hands, Twoface!' she chuckled.

She took another sip of Hedgehog Cola and peered back out the window at Shnozville High Street. 'Where IS everyone? It's been quiet in here all morning.'

A car floated past while a dog did a hover-poo on the pavement. 'I don't know what's going on,' she said. 'Nobody seems to want a Cheesebleurgher Meal Deal today . . .'

'Apart from us, Bunny!' I said to make her feel better. I took a sip on my avocado and felt-tip pen flavour soda, and the two little television aerials that've been sticking out of my head ever since I got zapped into the future did a wiggle.

The little black-and-white TV on my stomach started to fuzz and crackle, and Splorg peered at the screen.

# INSECTY RECTANGLE

'YOINKS! What's that weird-looking flying thing on your telly belly, Ratboy?' said Splorg, and I looked down at my stomach.

A hairy pointy-toothed insecty rectangle about half the size of Not Bird was flying straight towards the screen, as if it was about to burst out of my belly.

'Looks like something's up!' said Bunny, and I nodded, doing my superhero face, because whenever something flashes up on my telly belly, it means there's trouble.

All of a sudden, a bitey-looking insecty rectangle exackeely the same size as the one on my telly belly flew straight through the door of Bunny Deli.

'Hairy flying thing!' blurted Splorg, who's scared of hairy flying things. 'Argh! Keep it away from me!' He jumped out of his chair and ran into the little bathroom at the back of Bunny Deli. 'Has it gone yet?' he whimpered from behind the door.

The insect, which was pink and had a long curly nose, buzzed towards Jamjar's nostrils and opened its mouth. 'NOM NOM!' it growled.

'Arrrgh! Shoo, you annoying little beast!' said Jamjar, waggling her five arms in the air. 'Stop trying to bite my nose!' She picked up a zigzaggedy chip and waved it like a sword.

The chip bonked the insect on the head and it twirled round, darting in the direction of Not Bird's beak.

'NOT!' growled Not Bird, doing his scariest face, and the insect changed its mind, did a loop the loop and headed for the ratty full-stop blob on the end of MY nose.

# FULL-STOP NOSE BLOB

'Waaah, not my full-stop nose-blob!'
I cried, half trying to make everyone
laugh, half a tiny bit scared the insect
was about to bite it off.

25

The insect landed on the blob and opened its mouth, the way something does when it's about to bite someone's nose off.

OPERATION FLICK THE INSECT OFF MY NOSE!

I shouted in my superhero voice, flicking the insect, and it flew through the air and landed splat in the middle of Twoface's four eyes.

The insect shook its head and blinked, looking like it was working out which one of Twoface's two noses to bite first. 'NOM NOM!' it cackled, scuttling down towards the nostrils of the left one.

'Get off me you stupid little hairy pink rectangle!' growled Twoface, trying to sound like he wasn't scared.

'Ooh, what a lot of fuss and bother!' chuckled Bunny, walking back over to our table, still holding the cup of Hedgehog Cola.

The insect paused, its jaws wide open. Its eyes swivelled round to look at Bunny, and its long curly nose did a sniff. 'NOM NOM?' it squeaked, leaping off Twoface's left nose and flying out of Bunny Deli.

Twoface patted his hood-wings down and breathed a sigh of relief. 'See - nothing to worry about!' he said.

'H-how did you do that, Bunny?' said Splorg, poking his gigantic bald blue head round the bathroom door.

'Maybe he didn't like my perfume!' chuckled Bunny. 'Now, about that shopping list,' she said, and she nodded at the Floaty Note 6000.

# "CUP NOSE"

'What in the name of unkeelness are you doing with your cup, Splorg?' said Twoface, slurping on his drink.

It was ten minutes later and we were walking down Shnozville High Street, following the Floaty Note 6000 to get Bunny's bits.

That's one of the keel things about Floaty Note 6000s. They're not just floating shopping lists - they know the way to the shops, and loads of other things too.

'I'm protecting my hooter from that horrible little insect!' said Splorg, who'd slotted his empty cup over the end of his nose. 'Mmm, carpet flavour lemonade - smells even better than it tastes!'

Twoface thought for a second, then pulled a plastic ray-gun-shaped water pistol out of his pocket. 'Hey, I've just had the keelest idea!' he said.

He emptied the rest of his drink into a little hole in the top of the ray gun and slotted his empty cup on to the end of one of his noses.

BUNNY DELI

He looked over at my cup and grinned. 'Don't mind if I borrow this do you, Ratboy?' he said, snatching my avocado and felt-tip pen flavour soda and pouring the last gulp's worth down a passing drain (drains move around in the future, in case you didn't know).

'Hey, I was enjoying that!' I said, kicking Twoface up the bum as he slotted the cup over the end of his other nose.

Jamjar pushed her big round glasses up
her nose and rolled her eyes at us all.

'Ooh look, it's Dr Smell!' she said,
waving down the street at Dr Smell,
who was sweeping the bit of
pavement in front of his
perfume shop.

Dr Smell's perfume shop is where Bunny
buys her favourite perfume, 'Stonk'.

'Hello Dr Smell!' said Jamjar, and Dr Smell waggled his arms around, swatting the end of his nose.

'That's a weird way to wave,' said Twoface, squirting his ray gun into his mouth. 'Mmm, walnut and pavement flavour chocolate milk, my favourite!' he grinned.

I Future-Ratboy-zoomed my eyes in on Dr Smell and gasped.

# WHAT I WAS GASPING ABOUT

'Dr Smell isn't waving - he's trying to swat one of those insecty things away from his nose!' I said.

Splorg stared at the insect, which was blue this time and even bitier-looking than the one before. 'ANOTHER NOM NOM? IT'S AN INVASION!' he screamed, running off and hiding behind a bollard.

'NOT!' screeched Not Bird, following him like a Floaty Note 6000, except brown and circle-shaped and more furry.

Twoface pointed his ray gun in the direction of the insect. 'Stand back, Dr Smell!' he shouted. 'Take THIS, you naughty little NOM NOM!'

A jet of walnut and pavement flavour chocolate milk squirted past Dr Smell's ear at the exact same second the Nom Nom sunk its teeth into the tip of his nose.

screamed Dr Smell.

'NOM NOM!' growled the Nom Nom, and before you could say a word that takes about three seconds to say, it'd pulled its teeth back out of Dr Smell's nose and buzzed off.

'Nice shot, Twoface!' I laughed, as Jamjar ran up to Dr Smell.

'Are you all right, Dr Smell?' she said, peering at two tiny little bite marks just above his nostrils.

'I-I think so, Jamjar,' stuttered Dr Smell, dabbing his nose with a hanky. 'Not very lucky with this thing, am I?' he said, pointing at his hooter, and I rewound my brain to a few weeks earlier, when his nose had been chopped off and stolen by the evil Mr X.

# WHO IS MR X?

Here are some factoids about Mr X:

1. He is the evilest man in Shnozville.

2. He stomps around town inside a giant metal scorpion, zapping stuff with its tail.

3. He zapped the wheelie bin that transported me here from the past, and now it's disappeared, which means I might never get back home.

'Any luck finding your bin, Future Ratboy?' asked Dr Smell, stuffing his hanky back into his pocket, and I stared at the bite marks above his nostrils, thinking how they looked a bit like eyebrows. If his nostrils had been eyeholes. And the bite marks had been hairy.

'No, we haven't been able to find it at all,' I said sadly, imagining my mum and dad and little sister sitting on the sofa at home, wondering where I was.

Twoface kicked me up the bum, but in a nice way, and Jamjar pulled a turquoise plastic triangle out of her jacket pocket. She tapped it with one of her loads of fingers.

'I've been trying to locate Ratboy's bin with my Triangulator,' she said, looking down at the triangle. 'It seems Mr X's lasers discombobulated the bin's internal metrics. I reset the Triangulator's homing modules, but even that didn't do the trick!'

'I see . . .' said Dr Smell, his eyes staring blankly in front of him like he was watching TV, and the Floaty Note 6000 did a little cough to remind us about Bunny's shopping.

COUGH!

'Anywaaay . . .' said Twoface, squirting another splurt of walnut and pavement flavour chocolate milk into his mouth. 'I'd love to stand around here all day talking about bins, but we've got hand care products to buy.'

'Of course, don't let me stop you having your fun!' said Dr Smell, disappearing into his perfume shop, and we headed off down the street.

# THREE-HEADED DOG

I peered up at the sky, careful not to look at the suns. 'Still can't believe there are two suns here in the future!' I said, and Twoface rolled his eyes because he still can't believe that I still can't believe there are two suns.

Three Nom Noms - one yellow, one orange and one green - whizzed past on the other side of the street, stopping to bite a three-headed dog on its noses.

'They're everywhere!' whimpered a voice from behind a bollard and I spotted Splorg's cup-covered nose, sticking out like a sore thumb. Actukeely, not at all like a sore thumb. More like a nose with a cup stuck over the end of it.

I ran over to the bollard and jumped on top of it, Future-Ratboy-zooming my eyes around, trying to see where all the Nom Noms were coming from.

The two suns were shining in my eyes, and all I could see was a sky full of annoying-looking hairy rectangular silhouettes.

# TINDERBOX ALLEY

We followed the Floaty
Note 6000 across the
road and down the tiny
little side street, waggling
our hands in the air to
protect our noses from
all the Nom Noms.

'Tinderbox Alley,' said Twoface, reading what it said on a dirty old street sign. 'Never been down here before . . .'

The side street was about a centimetre narrower than the width of a hover-car, which meant there were no hover-cars going down it - only people. The buildings on either side zigzagged into the sky and each one had a tiny little shop at the bottom of it.

49

A man wearing a back-to-front hover-cap, a baggy white F-shirt* and really, really long shorts** was walking down the middle of the road with his arms stretched out in front of him like a zombie and his nose twitching in the air.

*F-shirts are for people whose arms are both on the same side.

**Actukeely, they were trousers.

'Hey, I've seen him in Bunny Deli loads of times!' said Jamjar, pushing her glasses up her nose for the eight-millionth time that day, and I wondered why she didn't invent a pair of glasses that didn't slide down her nose.

Just then an old lady in a hover-wheelchair vroomed past us, her eyes staring straight ahead.

'Doesn't she come into Bunny Deli sometimes too?' said Twoface.

Not Bird fluttered over to Splorg and landed on his head, which is something Not Bird likes to do.

# 'WAAAHHH!!! NOM NOM!!!'

screamed Splorg, running round in a circle like his ears were on fire. 'Let's get the keelness out of here!'

'Calm down, Splorgy Baby, it's only Not Bird!' I chuckled, as the Floaty Note 6000 floated up to a dingy, closed-looking shop.

'Harry's Handy Hand Shop,' said Jamjar, reading what it said on the sign above the door.

'Quick, before we all get chomped!' said Splorg, turning the handle, and the door creaked open.

# INSIDE THE SHOP

The shop was dark and smelt of doormats. Shelves sagged against the walls and I Future-Ratboy-opened my eyes extra wide, trying to see what was on them.

A single candle floated above an old wooden counter at the back of the room. Hovering next to it was one of those plastic globe things you shake to make the snow inside start swishing around.

# 'CAN'T... SEE... VERY... WELL...'

I said in my superhero voice and I darted my eyes around until I spotted a plug socket.

I plugged the plug on the end of my tail into it and the little TV screen on my belly flickered to life, lighting up the room.

'Looks like Floaty's found the perfect shop!' said Jamjar, pointing at a wall filled with thousands of different-coloured nail varnishes.

I swizzled my eyes two billimetres to the right and counted three hundred and seventy nine different tubes of hand cream, all crammed into one cabinet.

A sign saying **"SOAP"** in big red letters hung from the ceiling. Underneath, a pyramid of multicoloured soaps teetered up to the tips of my aerials.

Splorg wandered over to a ginormous metal chest with eight trillion tiny drawers and pulled one open.

'Gloves! Millions and billions of gloves!' he gasped.

The drawer was about a mile deeper than it looked from the outside and piled to the top with woolly brown gloves.

'Looking for anything in particular?' bubbled a tiny little voice from the direction of the counter and we all jumped a billimetre off the ground.

'Put your hands up!' shouted Twoface, whipping his ray gun out and pointing it at the snow globe.

# HARRY NO-HANDS

'If only I could!' bubbled the tiny little voice and I Future-Ratboy-zoomed my eyes in on the snow globe. Inside, floating upside down, was what looked like a mouldy piece of old chewed-up bubblegum. 'I'm afraid I haven't got any hands TO put up!' it said.

Jamjar pulled the Triangulator out of her pocket and pointed it at the snow globe. 'Hmmm ... seems to be some kind of germ-based extra-terrestrial life form,' she said, looking up at the little bubblegum man.

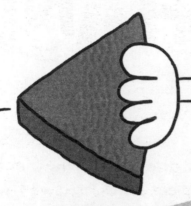

'Please, call me Harry!' chuckled the man, doing a loop the loop, and the snow inside his globe swirled around.

'Nice to meet you, Harry!' said Twoface, tucking his ray gun into his belt and holding his hand out for a shake. 'Oops, sorry!' he said, remembering what Harry had just said about not having any hands.

Splorg looked around to make sure there were no Nom Noms in the shop and pulled the cup off the end of his nose. 'Hope you don't mind me asking, but why did you open a HAND SHOP when you haven't got any hands?' he said.

'Great question!' said Harry. 'I come from the planet Kwagglethump – heard of it?'

# WE ALL SHOOK OUR HEADS.

'Doesn't matter. The thing about Kwagglethump? There's nothing on it!'

Not Bird floated over to a box of thimbles and slotted one on the end of his beak like a mini nose-protector.

'You know what happens when there's nothing on a planet?' said Harry and we all shook our heads again. 'There's nothing to pick up! You know what happens when there's nothing to pick up? You don't need hands!'

Twoface picked a nail file up off a shelf. 'Oh yeah . . . you DO need hands to pick stuff up, don't you!' he said and Jamjar rolled her eyes.

'Long story short,' said Harry, 'I came to Shnozville on a day trip. I couldn't believe it - so many things to pick up! Carrier bags, hamsters, muesli bars . . . the list is endless. Would you like me to go on?'

# WE SHOOK OUR HEADS AGAIN.

'So you opened a shop selling stuff for hands?' asked Splorg.

'You've gotta look after your grabbers when there's this many things to pick up,' said Harry, all seriously.

'And how's business?' asked Jamjar.

'Couldn't be better!' said Harry, looking around his shop proudly. 'Actukeely, it could be a BIT better. In fact, it couldn't be worse. Nobody EVER comes down this street!'

'THERE'S somebody!' said Splorg, pointing at a familikeels-looking person walking past outside.

'Hey, it's Dr Smell!' I said, waving to him, but he just carried on walking with his arms stretched out in front of him like a zombie, his nose twitching in the air.

'Ahem . . .' coughed the Floaty Note 6000, and Twoface clicked his fingers, remembering why we'd come in here in the first place.

CLICK!

'Ah yes, we'd like
a tube of hand cream,
a bottle of nail varnish and
a bar of soap please,' he said.

'I think I can manage that!'
beamed Harry.

# NINE HUNDRED BILLION POUNDS

'That'll be nine hundred billion pounds, please!' said Harry, once we'd tested every tube of hand cream, bottle of nail varnish and bar of soap in the shop.

'What a bargain!' said Splorg and the Floaty Note 6000 beeped itself against Harry's till. (The Floaty Note 6000 also pays for stuff, which is keel.)

Harry nodded at the cup in Splorg's hand. 'What's the cup for?' he said and Splorg held it up all proudly, like he was in an advert for a crumpled-up old cup.

It's my Nom Nom nose-protector!

said Splorg.

BUNNY DELI

'Nom Nom? What in the name of
Kwagglethump is a Nom Nom?'
said Harry.

'Haven't you seen them? There are
millikeels out there! Horrible little hairy
bitey rectangle things with curly noses,'
said Splorg, peering out the window.

Harry did a loop the loop inside his
snow globe. 'Oh, THOSE things! Yes,
there was one in here earlier!' he said.
'Didn't bother me, what with the
built-in protection and all,' he grinned,
bumping himself against the inside
of the globe.

'IN HERE? THERE WAS A NOM NOM IN HERE?' shrieked Splorg, dropping his cup, and it rolled underneath the counter.

Twoface whipped his ray gun out and I Future-Ratboy-darted my eyes around the shop. 'Don't worry Splorgy Baby, we've got this covered,' I said.

A tiny little bottle of nail varnish remover teetered forwards on the edge of a shelf.

'NOM NOM!' growled a voice and the bottle fell, crashing to the floor next to Jamjar's feet.

THERE, TWOFACE-THERE!

cried Jamjar, pointing all her fingers at a bright red Nom Nom.

'NOT!' screeched Not Bird, zooming at it with his thimble beak-protector on.

The Nom Nom leapt off the shelf, dodged Not Bird and darted towards Splorg.

'WAAAHHH!!!' screamed Splorg, heading for the door.

'Have a nice day!' shouted Harry, as I pulled my plug out of the socket and followed the gang out on to the street.

# TRIPPING OVER HOVER-POOS

'My nose-protector! I haven't got my nose-protector!' shrieked Splorg, zigzagging down Tinderbox Alley. The Nom Nom was zooming after him, its rectangle-shaped body stretched into a triangle from how fast it was flying.

Twoface pointed his ray gun at the Nom Nom and pulled the trigger, but nothing splurted out.

'Empty!' he cried. Not that the walnut and pavement flavour chocolate milk was going to do anything anyway.

'Faster, Splorg!' shouted Jamjar, who was carrying Bunny's bits in a 'Harry's Handy Hand Shop' carrier bag. 'The Nom Nom's catching you up!'

'Oh thanks a lot for that, Jamjar!' shouted Splorg over his shoulder, not spotting the hover-poo that was crossing the road. 'GAAAHHH!!!' he screamed, tripping over it and forward-rolling into the gutter.

Not Bird overtook the Nom Nom and skidded to a stop just in front of Splorg's nostrils. 'H-H-HELP MEEE!!!' wailed Splorg, scrabbling to his feet and stumbling down the road as Not Bird jabbed his beak-protector at the Nom Nom.

'OPERATION DO SOMETHING INSTEAD OF JUST WATCHING!' I shouted to myself in my superhero voice, and I grabbed hold of the Floaty Note 6000 and gave it a tug like a cowboy pulling on his horse's reigns.

The Floaty Note 6000 reared up, then shot forwards, dragging me through the air. 'YIPPEE-KEEL-KAYAY!' I cried, flying past Jamjar and Twoface. 'DON'T WORRY, SPLORGY BABY, FUTURE RATBOY'S HERE!'

# GIANT "ALIEN RAIN-DROP

You know how I'd just shouted, 'DON'T WORRY, SPLORGY BABY, FUTURE RATBOY'S HERE!'? Well I was too late because he'd already been bitten.

# OWW!!!

screamed Splorg, grabbing the end of his nose as the Nom Nom buzzed off.

'Splorg!' cried Jamjar. 'Does it hurt?'

'What in the unkeelness do you think?' said Twoface, running up and peering at the two little bite marks above Splorg's nostrils.

'I think I'm going to faint,' warbled Splorg, leaning against the window of the shop we were standing in front of, and he slid down the glass like a giant alien raindrop.

The Floaty Note 6000 floated over to Splorg and wafted air on to his face. 'Thanks Floaty, that's better,' whimpered Splorg.

Jamjar breathed a sigh of relief and looked up at the sign above the shop. 'X BURGER?' she said and I Future-Ratboy-zoomed my eyes through the window.

'HEY, DR SMELL'S IN THERE!'

I said.

Dr Smell was sitting at a table, tucking into a cheeseburger and chips. The cheeseburger had an 'X' stamped into the top of its bun and the chips were shaped like Xs.

Jamjar squidged her face against the glass. 'What in the name of unkeelness is Dr Smell doing in there?' she said. 'He usually gets his lunch at Bunny Deli!'

She peered up at the sign above the shop again. 'X BURGER. Hmmm, there's only ONE person who'd call their shop THAT!'

RGER

'Who?' whispered Twoface, and Jamjar rolled her eyes.

'Mr X, of course!' she said.

'Of course, Mr X!' said Twoface. 'It all makes perfect sense!'

I squidged my face up against the glass next to Jamjar's and twizzled my eyes around, looking at the other people inside the restaurant.

'No wonder Bunny Deli's been so empty. Everyone's in here!' I said, spotting the man with the back-to-front hover-cap and the old lady in the hover-wheelchair, too.

The walls were covered in posters of Mr X, smiling like he owned the place, which I spose he did.

Splorg grabbed on to the Floaty Note 6000 and pulled himself up. 'There's something very fishy about this,' he said, waggling his just-bitten nostrils. 'Or should I say . . . something very X BURGERY!'

'You're right, Splorg,' said Jamjar, pointing her Triangulator through the window and gasping. 'Oh my unkeelness, Ratboy - it's your bin!'

# "ROBOT" WAITER

'WHERE?' I cried, peering through the window of X BURGER, looking for my bin.

'THERE!' said Jamjar, pointing to the back of the little restaurant, and I spotted a wheelie bin wearing a white shirt, a black jacket and a bow tie. It had two plastic tube-arms with washing up gloves stuck on the end of them.

'That's not my bin!' I said. 'Mine was green, and it didn't look like some sort of robot waiter!'

'That must be why I've been having so much trouble locating it,' said Jamjar, tapping her plastic triangle. 'Not only did Mr X's lasers discombobulate the bin's internal metrics, it seems he confused my Triangulator's homing modules with some kind of cloaking device as well.'

## HUH?

said Twoface.

'Mr X dressed Ratboy's bin up in a suit to stop my Triangulator finding it!' said Jamjar.

'What I don't get is why Mr X would want to open a BURGER SHOP,' said Splorg and he licked his lips, his eyes fixed on Dr Smell's X BURGER.

'YE-AH!' said Twoface. 'Isn't he sposed to be an evil mastermind or something?'

Not Bird fluttered over to Splorg and sat on his head. 'Maybe he's had enough of being a baddy and fancied running a little restaurant instead?' said Splorg, and I rolled my eyes.

'As IF Mr X has had enough of being a baddy!' I said. 'Baddies don't EVER have enough of being bad! They just get older and grumpier and even more BADDIER!'

'So what IS he up to then, Ratboy?' said Twoface, and I scratched my full-stop nose-blob.

'I don't know,' I said. 'But I'm gonna get my bin back!'

# WHEELIE THE WAITER

'GOOD AFTERNOON AND WELCOME TO X BURGER!' bleeped my bin in a posh computery voice as we walked through the door. 'MY NAME IS WHEELIE AND I'LL BE YOUR WAITER TODAY!'

Jamjar peered at a circuit board
wired into the top of Wheelie's lid.
'Looks like Mr X fitted your bin with
some kind of speech module,' she said.

I walked up to the bin and held
my arms out for a hug. 'Wheelie!'
I beamed.

HELLO, SIR. WOULD YOU
LIKE TO TAKE A SEAT
AND I WILL FIND YOU
A HOVER-MENU

bleeped Wheelie, his lid flapping up and
down. A disgusting smell, sort of how
you'd imagine a bin's breath to stink,
wafted up my nostrils.

'D-don't you recognise me, Wheelie?'
I said, tiptoeing back from the stench.
'We were hit by lightning together and
zapped into the future, remember?
I got turned into a superhero rat!'

I pointed to my full-stop nose blob and
my superhero-ish black bin bag cape.

'I WOULDN'T KNOW ABOUT THAT, SIR,'
said Wheelie, wiping down a table
and pulling out a chair. 'PLEASE, TAKE
A SEAT!'

Dr Smell swallowed the last bite of his X BURGER and smiled at the bin. 'Waiter, that was excellent. Another one, please!' he said and the hover-menu fizzled a whole nother X BURGER to life in front of him.

'Shouldn't you be in Bunny Deli?' said Jamjar to Dr Smell.

'Ooh, hello Jamjar!' said Dr Smell, pulling a little bottle of 'Stonk for Men' out of his inside jacket pocket and spraying it under his armpits. 'I see you've found this place too - fantastic, isn't it!'

'Best burgers in town,' spluttered the man with the hover-cap on. His mouth was full of X BURGER, and X CHIPS were sticking out of it like little arms trying to get free.

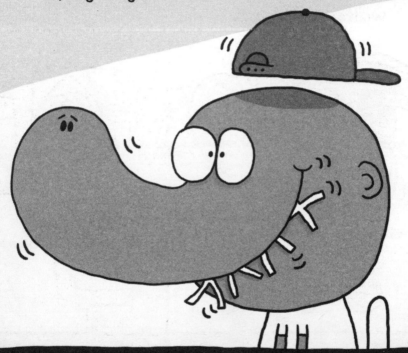

Jamjar pointed her Triangular at the hover-cap man's mouth. 'That's funny,' she said. 'This food is made out of one hundred and twelve per cent cardboard!'

'Mmm, cardboardy delishy-wishy-ness!'
cackled the old lady in the hover-
wheelchair, stuffing her last X CHIP
into her mouth. Her eyes were staring
blankly in front of her, like she was
watching TV.

'ANYWAAAY . . .' I said, trying to
change the subject. 'Shall we head
off, Wheelie?'

'HEAD OFF, SIR? I'M NOT SURE WHAT
YOU MEAN,' bleeped my bin, smellily.

I pointed to the door. 'Well, it's all very keel being in the future and everything, but I'm gonna HAVE to go home at some point. My mum and dad'll be wondering where I am!'

Wheelie stared at me, or at least pointed his lid in my direction. 'I HAVEN'T THE FAINTEST IDEA WHAT YOU'RE TALKING ABOUT, SIR,' he said in his computery voice.

'You're my magic bin!' I said, getting a bit annoyed. 'I need you to zap me back to the past!'

'PERHAPS A NICE CUP OF X-TEA WOULD CALM YOU DOWN, SIR?' said Wheelie. 'X-TRA LARGE, I THINK!'

'I don't want a cup of X-TEA, I want to go HOME!' I cried, grabbing Wheelie by the handle, and he yelped.

## GET YOUR HANDS OFF ME THIS INSTANT!

he bleeped, zooming off in the direction of a metal door at the back of the shop.

# RUN FOR IT!

The metal door at the back of X BURGER whooshed upwards and Wheelie zoomed through it, into a tiny silver room.

I peered across the restaurant into the room and spotted TV screens all over the walls, surrounded by billions of different-shaped buttons.

'Right, that's it - no more Mr Nice Ratboy!' I said, stomping towards Wheelie. 'You're coming with me whether you like it or not!'

Wheelie twizzled round on his wheels and opened his lid wide. A deep rumbling noise echoed out of his insides, and his arms raised into the air, like someone had tied balloons to his washing-up gloves.

'RELEASE THE INSECTS!' he boomed and a swarm of multicoloured Nom Noms floated out of him like an evil stinking rainbow.

'N-N-N-N-NOM-NOMS!!!' screamed
Splorg, diving towards the front door.
'They're coming out of Ratboy's bin!'

'RUN FOR IT!' cried Twoface, pointing
at a metal shutter, which had started
to judder downwards from the ceiling.

'But what about my bin?' I cried.

'Forget your smelly bin, Ratboy!'
shouted Jamjar, grabbing my arm and
dragging me across the floor.

'NOT!' screeched Not Bird, pecking at the NOM NOMS with his thimble-covered beak.

Splorg stared over his shoulder at Dr Smell's X BURGER, then dived through the front door, Twoface forward-rolling after him.

'Follow me!' cried Jamjar, sliding under the shutter, and I glanced across the restaurant towards the tiny room at the back.

The metal door had half whooshed down and I could see Wheelie frantically pressing all the buttons to lock himself in.

'Stay here with us, Ratface!' cackled the old lady, sinking her teeth into her X BURGER, and Dr Smell nodded.

'Yes - join us, Ratboy!' he grinned. He reached his arms out towards me like a zombie and I twizzled round.

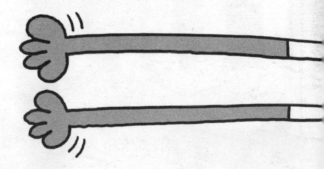

'OPERATION GET THE KEELNESS OUT OF HERE!' I cried, grabbing hold of Not Bird in one hand and the Floaty Note 6000 in the other, and I forward-rolled through the front door, out on to the street.

# NOT BIRD'S LUNCH

'This way!' shouted Twoface. He ran to the end of Tinderbox Alley and jumped on to a wall, his nose-protectors falling off his noses as he tumbled over it.

I looked behind me and spotted a cloud of multicoloured Nom Noms zooming towards us through the air. 'NOT!' squawked Not Bird, waggling his thimble beak-protector off his beak.

He flew up to the Nom Noms and opened his mouth. 'NOM . . . nom?' screeched the Nom Nom at the front, disappearing into Not Bird's mouth.

'Looks like somebody's ready for their lunch!' cried Jamjar, jumping over the wall with Splorg as Not Bird flew forwards and swallowed the whole cloud.

'Exkeelent work, Not Bird!' I said, scrabbling up the wall. 'OOF!' I blurted, tumbling over it and looking around.

# "THE OLD" PLAYGROUND

We'd landed in an old-fashioned playground, a bit like the ones I used to go to with my mum and dad and little sister when I was Colin Lamppost.

There was a slide, a roundabout, two swings and a seesaw. All of them were rusty and paint-chipped and didn't look like they were from the future at all.

In the corner of the playground stood
a scuffed-up old vending machine,
stacked full of mouldy-looking snacks.

'Now what?' said Splorg, standing up
and dusting himself down. Not that
there's any dust in the future.

'I've got to get my bin back!' I cried,
plonking my bum down on a swing and
trying to come up with a plan.

'What are you, CRAZY, Ratboy?' said Twoface, climbing the ladder to the top of the slide and zooming down it head first. 'Did you see what came out of that thing?'

Jamjar gave the roundabout a shove and jumped on. 'Twoface is right, Ratboy - it's too dangerous to go back to X BURGER,' she said, the roundabout squeaking round and round.

'Come on you lot, are you scaredy cats or something?' I said. 'Don't you wanna find out what's going on with Dr Smell?'

Splorg stroked the end of his nose where the Nom Nom had bitten it. 'It WAS a bit . . . unusual . . . in there, wasn't it,' he said. His eyes had glazed over, the way mine do when I'm thinking about what I'm going to eat for tea.

'I've been thinking about that too,' said Jamjar, pushing her glasses up her nose.

'Why in the keelness would Dr Smell want to eat a cardboard flavour burger when Bunny's are so delishy-wishious? It doesn't make any sense!'

'Mr X is up to something, that's for sure!' said Twoface, as Not Bird sat on one end of the seesaw and it clunked to the ground from the weight of all the Nom Noms in his belly.

CLUNK!

'Erm, I don't want to interfere or anything, but perhaps I could be of assistance?' warbled a friendly old voice coming from the corner of the playground, and we all turned round to face it.

# "THE WISE OLD VENDING MACHINE

There in the corner of the playground
stood the vending machine.

'That thing looks way too old to have a speech module,' said Jamjar, walking over to it. She whipped her Triangulator out, slid one of its corners into the vending machine's coin slot and pressed a few buttons.

'A-ha, looks like it was modified back in the seven millionth century!'

Twoface walked over and peered through the vending machine's scratched-up window at the mouldy snacks inside. 'Did you say something, Mr Vending Machine?' he asked, tapping on the glass.

'I couldn't help overhearing you talking about X BURGER,' chimed the vending machine, his flap swinging open and shut all squeakily. 'Maybe I can help? My name's not Mr Vending Machine, by the way. It's The Wise Old Vending Machine.'

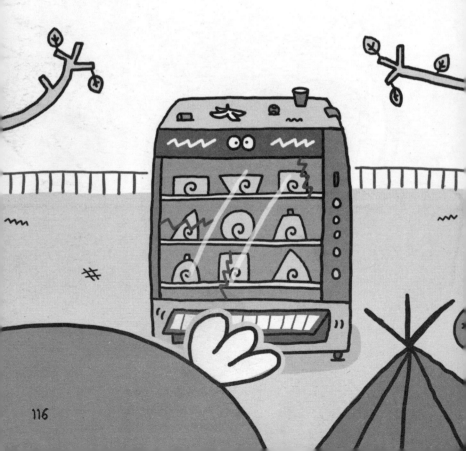

'Oh. Nice to meet you, The Wise Old Vending Machine,' said Twoface. 'We just came from X BURGER. Dr Smell and some other weirdos were having their lunch inside. Which is strange, because they usually go to Bunny Deli.'

The light bulb inside The Wise Old Vending Machine flickered as he listened.

'Not only that, but Ratboy's wheelie bin was the waiter!' said Jamjar.

Splorg sat on the seesaw opposite Not Bird. 'Anyone else feeling peckish?' he said, licking his lips.

NOT BUDGING

I looked at Not Bird to see if he thought it was weird that there was a talking vending machine having a chat with Twoface and Jamjar, but he didn't seem that bothered.

'Now Wheelie's locked himself in a room at the back of the restaurant and we can't get him out,' said Twoface. 'And without Wheelie, Ratboy won't be able to zap himself home!'

The Wise Old Vending Machine nodded as Twoface pressed one of the buttons on his front.

A packet of mouldy crisps whirred off a ledge behind his window and dropped into the little compartment behind his flap. 'Ooh, crisps!' grinned Twoface, sticking his hand through the flap and grabbing them.

'I'd give those a miss if I were you,'
chimed The Wise Old Vending Machine.
'They went off in 1987.'

'How long have you been here, exactly?'
said Twoface, placing the crisps on top
of The Wise Old Vending Machine like
a little crinkly hat.

'Let's just say sales haven't been good
for the last few million years or so,'
said The Wise Old Vending Machine.
'Now, about getting this bin back –
have you thought about using one of
the Ancient Giant Worm Tunnels?'

# ANCIENT GIANT WORM TUNNELS

'What in the name of unkeelness are the Ancient Giant Worm Tunnels?' said Twoface.

The Wise Old Vending Machine smiled. Or at least he swung his flap open and shut. 'There are Ancient Giant Worm Tunnels all over Shnozville,' he said.

He looked over at a manhole cover in the ground next to him.

'They're left over from the Ancient Giant Worms. There's bound to be one that leads to the little room at the back of X BURGER.'

'Giant worms?' said Splorg, and Not Bird's ears pricked up. Not that he's exackeely GOT ears.

'Yes, didn't you know?' said The Wise Old Vending Machine. 'Shnozville was ruled by giant worms from the planet CLORGLEFLUMP for thousands of years. They lived underground most of the time, in their giant wormholes. There's still a few of them alive down there, apparently!'

'NOT!' squawked Not Bird, looking all excited at the thought of a giant worm for pudding, and we all had a good chuckle, until Twoface suddenly stopped chuckling and did his serious faces.

'Hang on a millikeels, why are we all chuckling?' he said. 'It's not like we actukeely WANT to climb through a giant worm tunnel and pop out into a tiny room with a crazy bin waiter inside it waiting to kill us all with Nom Noms, is it?'

Splorg stopped chuckling too. 'Twoface has a point,' he said. 'Shall we just stay here and play on the swings instead?'

'Urgh, and you call yourselves superheroes?' I said.

'Actually, that's just Twoface,' said Splorg, his eyes staring blankly in front of him like he was watching TV.

I turned to Jamjar, who was standing next to the manhole cover, her glasses beginning to slide down her nose.

'It's not just about me getting home,'
I said. 'We've got to find out what's
making Bunny's customers want to eat
X BURGERS instead of cheesebleurghers!
If we don't, Bunny Deli will close down
– and then what'll happen to poor
old Bunny?'

Jamjar whipped her Triangulator out
and prised the manhole cover open
with it. She poked her nose into the
hole and peered up at Twoface and
Splorg.

'I can't believe I'm saying this, but
Ratboy's right,' she said. 'We have
to help Bunny!'

# SOMETHING X BURGERY GOING ON

'Take care down there, kiddywinkles,'
warbled The Wise Old Vending Machine
as we lowered ourselves down the
ladder and pulled the manhole cover
over our heads. 'Watch out for the
giant worms!'

'Dark down here, isn't it,' said Splorg, waggling his nose. 'Something smells goooood though!'

'I can't smell anything,' said Twoface, as I looked around for a plug socket to plug my plug into.

'If only I could light up my telly belly,' I mumbled. 'It's SO annoying that it only lights up when my tail is plugged in. Or when somebody in trouble flashes up on its screen . . .'

'WAY too much information, Ratboy!' said Twoface, doing a fake yawn, and Jamjar giggled.

'Floaty - activate glow-mode!' she smiled, and the Floaty Note 6000 started to fizzle bright yellow and light up the blackness.

We walked forwards five steps and came to a fork. I don't mean a fork for eating with. I mean a fork in the tunnel, when there's two ways to go and you don't know which one to take.

Then I looked down and saw an ACTUAL REAL LIFE fork, just lying on the ground, all bent and muddy. Not that I had time to wonder how THAT got there.

# OPERATION TRY AND WORK OUT WHICH WAY TO GO!

I said in my superhero voice as Splorg walked straight past me, breathing in through his nostrils.

X BURGERs – that's what I can smell! Follow me, gang!

he said, heading round the corner, down the tunnel to the right.

Jamjar pulled her Triangulator out and pointed it at Splorg. 'Hmmm, there's something fishy going on here,' she whispered, so Splorg couldn't hear. 'Or should I say . . .

# SOMETHING X BURGERY!'

'Yeah, how can he smell X BURGERS when they're one hundred and twelve per cent cardboard?' I said. 'Cardboard doesn't SMELL!'

And that was when there was a weird noise.

# FLUUURGH!!!

went the noise.

'Er, did you hear that noise?' I said.

'NOT!' screeched Not Bird, but only
because he hasn't really got ears.

# FLUUURGH!!!

went the noise again.

'What IS that?' said Twoface,
pulling out his ray gun.

# FLUUURGH!!!
### went the noise AGAIN.

'Oh, guy-uys . . . you might want to
take a look at this,' said Splorg, and
we all peered round the corner.

# GIANT WORM

'G-g-giant worm!' cried Jamjar, dropping her Triangulator, and it bounced along the floor towards the giant worm that was filling the tunnel with its disgusting face.

The worm had seventeen eyes, all of them glowing red. Two pairs of shiny black claws snipped at the air, and its teeth dripped with browny-yellow drool.

'FLUUURGGGH!!!' roared the worm, snaffling up the Triangulator.

'My Triangulator!' shrieked Jamjar,
running past Splorg towards the giant
worm's mouth.

'Jamjar, NOOOOO!!!' I cried, as the
giant worm's mouth opened to the
width of the tunnel and swallowed
Jamjar whole.

Splorg turned round. His black eyeballs
had turned grey. 'We have to do
something!' he squeaked.

'B-b-but the worm!' stuttered
Twoface, tiptoeing backwards.

'As long as we make it past the teeth
we should be OK,' I said, even though
I was only really guessing. 'The rest is
just worm-insides!'

Splorg waggled his nostrils and took a long sniff. 'Plus X BURGER is at the end of this tunnel!' he shouted. 'We HAVE to go through the worm to get to it!'

'NOT!' screeched Not Bird and Twoface at the same time, and I stepped forwards and put my hands on my hips, superhero style.

140

# OPERATION SAVE JAMJAR!

I shouted, tucking Not Bird under my arm and grabbing Splorg's and Twoface's hands. I bit the corner of the Floaty Note 6000 and crossed my ratty toes.

## GIDDY UP, FLOATY!

I cried and the Floaty Note 6000 zoomed forwards through the air, dragging us straight into the mouth of the giant worm.

# INSIDE THE GIANT WORM

'See, I told you it wouldn't be so bad!' said Twoface, pretending he hadn't been scared. It was three billiseconds later and we were squelching our way through the worm.

It was sort of the same as being in the tunnel, except squidgier. The walls were all rubbery and drips of wormy-smelling goo dribbled from the wobbly ceiling above our heads.

'Jamjar, where are you?' I cried.

'Yeurgh! It's like being inside a giant nostril!' said Splorg, twitching his own tiny little ones.

I'M DOWN HERE!

called Jamjar, her voice muffled by the meaty worm walls.

'Oh this is just fantastikeels,' said Twoface. 'All we did was pop out for a few bits, and now we're in the middle of a giant worm on our way to have a fight with a robot bin!'

'I know, exciting isn't it!' I said, treading on what looked like a half-chewed-up hover-poo.

We turned a corner inside the worm and spotted Jamjar. 'Found it!' she grinned, pulling her arm out of a brown jellyish ball of slime and holding up the Triangulator.

'Brillikeels. Can we get the unkeelness out of here now, please?' said Twoface.

'This way,' said Jamjar, pointing at a hole that was opening and closing. 'We just have to get through the intestines!'

# MANHOLE COVER

'Well that was lovely,' said Twoface, plopping out of the giant worm's bum and landing on the tunnel floor.

'Anyone need a handy wipe?' said Splorg, scraping a splodge of worm poo off his forehead with the Floaty Note 6000 and passing it to me.

The Floaty Note 6000 looked at me, or at least pointed its writing side in my direction. 'I'm all right thanks,' I said, feeling a bit sorry for it.

'Hey, look at this!' said Jamjar, pointing to a ladder leading up to a manhole cover.

There were some strange letters dented into the underneath side of the cover.

'REGRUB X?' said Twoface, reading them out loud.

'Maybe it's some kind of ancient giant worm language?' I said, trying to sound clever.

'Language smanguage. Who can smell X BURGERS?' said Splorg, sounding excited.

'X BURGER! That's it!' said Jamjar, clicking two of her fingers.

EH?

said Twoface.

'The manhole cover - it says
X BURGER, but back to front!' said
Jamjar, and I Future-Ratboy-flipped
my eyeballs round so they could read
in reverse.

'X BURGER!' cried Twoface, copying
what Jamjar had just said. 'It says
X BURGER, but back to front!'

# JAMJAR WORKS IT OUT

Jamjar heaved the manhole cover open and we peeked our heads up through the hole into the tiny silver room at the back of X BURGER.

'This is it! It must be Mr X's control room,' said Jamjar, looking around.

'All clear,' said Twoface, climbing out of the hole and glancing about. 'Looks like Wheelie sneaked back into the restaurant once we left!'

'Oh brilliant,' I said, looking at the locked metal door. 'I just climbed through a giant worm for nothing!'

As well as all the TV screens and different-shaped buttons I'd seen on the walls earlier, there was also a small dingy window on the side of the room that faced the restaurant.

'Hey look, there's Dr Smell! I can't believe he's STILL here,' said Twoface, peering through the little window.

Dr Smell was sitting at his table, biting into another X BURGER. Wheelie was wheeling around the restaurant, picking up empty wrappers and wiping tables. 'Twoface, get down!' I cried. 'Wheelie'll spot you!'

'Don't worry, Ratboy,' said Jamjar. 'It's a two-way mirror. I spotted it when we were in X BURGER earlier - this side's a window and the other is a reflective surface.'

'Oh, that's OK then,' I said, trying to play it keel, and Twoface scratched his two heads.

'Hang on a millikeels, Ratboy. What exackeely IS your plan for getting that bin of yours back?' he said. 'Because it feels to me like you're a teeny weeny bit TERRIFIED of Wheelie right now!'

'Oh, er . . . I'm not exackeely sure yet,' I said, darting my eyes around the room, trying to come up with a superhero-ish idea.

'Mmm, smell those X BURGERS!' said Splorg, tiptoeing up to the wall to see through the little window. 'I could eat a hundred!' he drawled, as Jamjar whipped her Triangulator out and pointed it at the end of his nose.

'How are you feeling, Splorg?' she said, tapping the plastic turquoise triangle. 'Any dizziness?' She'd stepped right up close to him and was squinting at the bite marks above his nostrils.

Splorg carried on staring through the window into X BURGER, which was full up now with people tucking into cardboardy meal deals.

'Never better!' said Splorg. 'Just need to get my hands on one of those delishy-wishy-looking X BURGERS,' he drooled.

'Mmm-hmm,' said Jamjar, looking through the window herself, then back at Splorg.

She tapped her Triangulator and closed
her eyes, looking like she was doing a
sum or something.

'What're you thinking, Jamjar?' I said,
and just as I said it she opened her
eyes and the Triangulator dropped out
of her hand.

'Oh my unkeelness,' she said, turning to
me, Twoface and Not Bird. 'I think I've
worked out what's going on here . . .'

# "JAMJAR EXPLAINS "WHAT "SHE'S "WORKED "OUT

'What? What have you worked out?' said Twoface. He was sitting on a hover-swivel-chair, fiddling with some of the buttons on the wall.

'It's the Nom Noms!' said Jamjar,
backing away from Splorg a bit. Splorg
didn't seem to notice though - he was
too busy staring through the little
window at all the cardboard burgers.

'NOT!' screeched Not Bird, and Jamjar
carried on explaining.

'Don't you see,' she said, pointing at Splorg's bite marks and then through the window. 'Everyone in X BURGER's been bitten by a Nom Nom!'

I Future-Ratboy-zoomed my eyes in on Dr Smell's nose, and the hover-cap man's, and the old lady's too. Jamjar was right - they all had little bite marks above their nostrils.

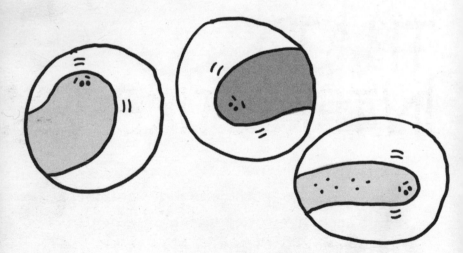

'There must be something about the Nom Nom bites that's making people want to eat X BURGERS!' said Jamjar.

'No wonder poor old Splorgy Baby's been acting so strange,' I said, and Twoface nodded, leaning forwards to look at a screen that was on the wall in front of where he was sitting.

# 'HEY, THAT'S INTERESTIKEELS,'

he said.

'Is that all you've got to say?' said Jamjar. 'Our best friend is turning into a zombie, and you're more interested in a stupid TV screen!'

Twoface swivelled round in his chair. 'I'm just trying to work out what in the name of unkeelness is going on,' he said, pointing at the screen. 'Now look at THIS!'

An image of a rotating Nom Nom had popped up on the screen, with the words 'OPERATION SHNOXVILLE' written above it.

'SHNOXVILLE?' said Jamjar. 'What in the unkeelness is SHNOXVILLE?'

Just below the screen was a little slot, about the width of Jamjar's Triangulator. 'Hmmm . . .' said Jamjar, pushing her Triangulator into the slot and crossing all her fingers. 'This is a long shot, but it might just work,' she said, pulling the triangle back out and peering down at it.

# BINGO!

she grinned.

# OPERATION SHNOX-VILLE

'Bingo WHAT?' said Twoface, and Jamjar looked up from her Triangulator.

'That little slot on the wall is an Information Decodifying Ziode,' she said. 'By inserting my Triangulator, I was able to read the variables on its circuit perambulator!'

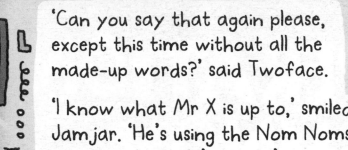

'Can you say that again please, except this time without all the made-up words?' said Twoface.

'I know what Mr X is up to,' smiled Jamjar. 'He's using the Nom Noms to control people's minds!'

'How do you mean?' I said.

'When a person gets bitten by a
Nom Nom they're injected with a tiny
microchip,' said Jamjar, tapping on
her triangle. 'It's that microchip that
makes them want to eat X BURGERS!'

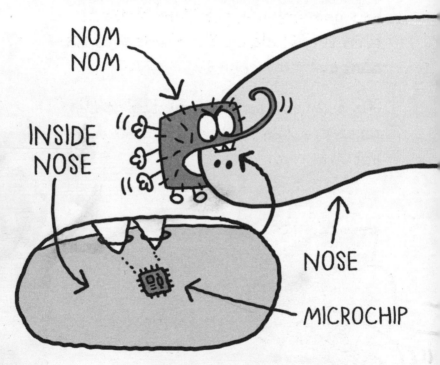

Twoface scratched one of his noses.
'So what's 'OPERATION SHNOXVILLE'
all about then?' he said.

'OPERATION SHNOXVILLE is Mr X's REAL plan,' said Jamjar, her face going all serious. 'X BURGERS are just the beginning. Once he knows he can make people do whatever he likes, he's going to use the Nom Noms to turn the whole of Shnozville into his own evil playground!'

She pointed her Triangulator at the screen on the wall and pressed a button on it.

The rotating Nom Nom disappeared and was replaced by a map of SHNOXVILLE.

'It's like Shnozville, except all X-ified!'
I cried, peering at the screen.

'All the buildings have got Xs on them!'
said Twoface, which was exackeely
what I'd just said, except ever so
slightly different.

'That's right, Twoface - all the shops
in SHNOXVILLE will be X SHOPS and
everyone will work for Mr X!'

'So what will Mr X be doing while everyone's busy taking care of his evil empire?' I said, and Jamjar pointed at the middle of the map. 'Hey, isn't that where the old playground is?' I said, trying to spot the swings and the roundabout and The Wise Old Vending Machine. But all I could see was a giant silver X-shaped building with tiny mirrored windows all over it.

'Not if Mr X gets his way,' said
Jamjar, pressing another
button on her Triangulator. 'That's
where his evil headquarters will be,' she
said and the screen zoomed in on the
X building and through one of its
windows.

Mr X was inside, sitting on a giant
X-shaped sofa. A servant with tiny
little bite marks above her nostrils
was feeding him X-shaped grapes.

Me and Twoface looked at each other and gasped. 'We have to kill the Nom Noms!' we said, both at exackeely the same time.

Jamjar pushed her glasses up her nose. 'The only problem is, I'm not sure that'll do the trick,' she said.

# SEE-THROUGH WHEELIE

'What do you mean?' I said, as Jamjar pressed a button on her Triangulator and an image of Wheelie popped up on the screen.

'The Nom Noms are all coming from one place,' said Jamjar. She pressed another button and one whole side of Wheelie turned see-through, so we could see inside him.

There, sitting in the bottom of Wheelie, was a Nom Nom about three times the size of the others. 'That is the Nom Nom Queen,' said Jamjar, and we all tiptoed a billimetre backwards.

The Nom Nom Queen was sitting on a pile of rotten food with a transparent pulsating sack of Nom Nom eggs hanging off her bum.

'No wonder Wheelie's breath stinks!' said Twoface, looking at a tiny hole at the end of the egg sack that was opening and closing.

Grub-like baby Nom Noms plopped out of the hole and burrowed into the rotten food, appearing seconds later as fully-grown biting rectangles. 'That is the most disgustikeels thing I have EVER seen,' said Twoface. 'And I just crawled out of a giant worm's bum!'

Jamjar looked at us. 'The only way to neutralise the extemporaneal diagrammatic is to obliterate the singularity axis,' she said.

# WE BOTH STARED AT HER, DOING OUR CONFUSED FACES.

'If we kill the Nom Nom Queen, the Noms Noms will all die!' she explained.

'Well then, let's kill the Nom Nom Queen!' I said and Jamjar scratched her forehead, which made a change from pushing her glasses up her nose I spose.

'The problem is, how are we going to do that without destroying Wheelie at the same time?' she said.

'Destroy Wheelie?' I said. 'We can't destroy Wheelie! If we destroy Wheelie I'll be stuck in the future FOREVER!'

I rewound my brain to the beginning of the day and pressed play, trying to see if anything had happened that might give me an idea.

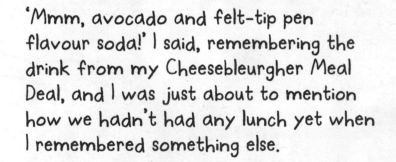

'Mmm, avocado and felt-tip pen flavour soda!' I said, remembering the drink from my Cheesebleurgher Meal Deal, and I was just about to mention how we hadn't had any lunch yet when I remembered something else.

'Wait a billisecond,' I said, pausing my brain on the bit when the Nom Nom had flown into Bunny Deli that morning. 'Bunny's perfume!' I cried. 'It's the Stonk! We have to get some Stonk!'

# IT'S NOT THE STONK

Jamjar and Twoface stared at me, doing their confused faces.

'Remember this morning, when Bunny got rid of the Nom Nom?' I said.

# THEY BOTH NODDED.

'Well, remember what she said afterwards?' I said.

# THEY BOTH SHOOK THEIR HEADS.

Maybe he didn't like my perfume!

I said, saying what Bunny had said.

'So what are you saying?' said Twoface, and Jamjar sighed.

'What Ratboy is saying, Twoface, is that maybe we could kill the Nom Nom Queen by spraying her with Stonk,' said Jamjar. 'That's what you're saying, right?' she said.

# I NODDED.

Twoface laughed. 'OK then, genius, answer me this - if the Nom Noms are so scared of Stonk, how come Dr Smell's got a Nom Nom bite on his hooter? Everyone knows he wears Stonk!'

I stared through the window at Dr Smell tucking into his X BURGER and remembered him spraying his armpits with a bottle of Stonk for Men earlier that day.

'A-ha, but he wears Stonk for MEN!' I said.

'Oh come on Ratboy, EVERYONE knows Stonk for Men is EXACKEELY the same as Stonk for Women!' chuckled Twoface, and I gave him one of my evil superhero stares, because everyone DOES know that.

I folded my arms across my telly belly and pressed play inside my head, looking for another clue.

'Perhaps Ratboy is on to something though,' said Jamjar all slowly, and I immedikeely pressed pause. 'Maybe it WAS something Bunny was wearing that scared the Nom Nom off . . .'

The little silver room we were standing in went quiet as we all tried to think. All of us except Splorg that is, who still had his face pressed up against the dingy window. 'Mmm, X BURGERS!' he drooled. 'THAT'S IT, I'M GOING IN!'

He reached for a yellow button I hadn't spotted before, next to the door to the restaurant. 'NO! You can't go out there, Splorg!' I cried. 'If Wheelie sees us now he'll release one of his evil stinky Nom Nom rainbows!'

'Who cares – Splorgy Baby's already been bitten!' smiled Splorg, pressing the button, and the door let out a wheeze.

'WAIT! I'VE GOT IT!' I cried. 'It's Bunny's hand care products! That's what scared the Nom Nom off!'

# NOT THAT EITHER

'I'VE GOT IT! It's Bunny's hand care products!' cried Twoface, copying exackeely what I'd just said. 'That's what scared the Nom Nom off this morning!'

'Hey, that was my idea!' I said, but Jamjar just ignored me.

'Nice idea, Twoface,' said Jamjar as the door to X BURGER started to whoosh upwards. 'But it doesn't quite add up.'

'Yeah, nice try, Twoface!' I said, pretending it wasn't my idea after all.

'How do you mean "doesn't quite add up"?' said Twoface, pulling out his ray gun and pointing it in the direction of the door, even though it was empty.

Jamjar held up her Harry's Handy Hand Shop carrier bag with Bunny's hand cream, nail varnish and soap inside. 'We tried all these out in the shop, remember? And it's not like the Nom Noms haven't been trying to bite us!'

HARRY'S
HANDY
HAND SHOP

Twoface stomped his foot on the floor. 'GAAAHHH!!! What WAS it then?' he cried.

The door had fully whooshed open now, even though I was pressing every button I could reach to make it close.

'Ah, hello again, gang!' smiled Dr Smell, turning around in his seat.

Wheelie, who was wiping down a table, stopped wiping it down and twizzled round on his wheels. 'INVADERS!' he bleeped, his lid flapping up and down.

'I tell you what, kids, this cardboard flavour soda is the bee's knees!' grinned Dr Smell, holding up his drink cup and taking a slurp, and I gasped.

'OK, this time I really HAVE cracked it!' I cried.

# "OK, THIS REALLY IS IT"

'Hedgehog Cola!' I shouted, as Wheelie started to open his lid. 'It was Jamjar's Hedgehog Cola!'

I forward-rolled into the restaurant and crouched behind the old lady in the hover-wheelchair's hover-wheelchair. 'What about it, Ratboy?' said Jamjar, who was hiding just inside the door to the little silver room, tapping away on her Triangulator.

Splorg had sat down at the table with the hover-cap man and was reading a hover-menu.

Twoface speed-crawled out of the little room on all fours, over to where I was crouching. 'Yeah Ratboy, what about Jamjar's Hedgehog Cola?' he whispered.

'Maybe the Hedgehog Cola was what frightened the Nom Nom off this morning!' I whispered back. 'Bunny was holding it in one of her hands, remember? If we could somehow fizzle up a cup of it, all we'd have to do is pour it into Wheelie!'

Twoface clicked his fingers. 'Hey, I think I've got it!' he grinned. 'Maybe the Hedgehog Cola was what frightened the Nom Nom off this morning!'

'Can you please stop copying every thing I say!' I cried, but Twoface just ignored me and carried on grinning.

'I don't know, Twoface. It's a long shot,' said Jamjar, and I sighed, looking up at Wheelie, who was waggling his arms in the air.

'It's not like anyone's come up with a better idea,' I said. 'Plus we're running out of time!'

# RELEASE THE NOM NOMS!

boomed Wheelie as his insides rumbled, and a trillion Nom Noms started to float out of his belly.

# "ORDERING HEDGEHOG COLA

'Now, what shall I have?' said Splorg, peering at the hover-menu.

'Jamjar, you're the Hedgehog Cola expert. Place an order - and quick!' I said.

'Fingers crossed!' said Jamjar. 'Hover-menu, I'd like an X BURGER Meal Deal, please.'

'What about the Hedgehog Cola?' I cried, as Jamjar squidged her face up.

'That's what I'm trying to think of!' she said. 'Remember, at Bunny Deli you get whatever drink you're THINKING OF when you place your order!'

An X BURGER Meal Deal fizzled to life on the table in front of Splorg and his nostrils waggled. 'Mmm, fandabbykeelkeels!' he cried, whipping the X BURGER out of its box and taking a bite.

I grabbed the drink cup and plopped the lid off, giving it a sniff. 'Poowee, what's that?' I said, looking at the brown, sludgy liquid inside.

'Porcupine Cola, as requested!' bleeped the hover-menu.

'Ooh, nearly!' I cried, and Jamjar sighed.

'Hover-menu, I'd like an X BURGER Meal Deal,' she said again, scrunching up her face, and another X BURGER Meal Deal fizzled to life on the table.

'This is my lucky day!' giggled Splorg, as I grabbed the cup and plopped off the lid.

'Poowee times twowee!' I cried.

'Anteater Cola, as you wished, madam!' bleeped the hover-menu, as a bright green Nom Nom hovered towards me, licking its lips.

'GAAAHHH!!! That's not even close, Jamjar!' said Twoface, and Jamjar closed her eyes and took a breath, long enough for the bright green Nom Nom to reach my nose and for me to swat it away.

'Hover-menu, I'd like an X BURGER Meal Deal,' she said and a third X BURGER Meal Deal fizzled to life on the table.

Jamjar grabbed the cup and plopped off the lid. 'YUCK - Hedgehog Cola!' she smiled as Twoface whipped his ray gun out of his pocket and opened the little hole in the top of it.

'Quick, pour it in here!' said Twoface, and Jamjar tilted the cup all shakily. 'Let's see how you stupid little hairy rectangles like THIS!' he said, as a giant metal scorpion screeched to a halt in the street outside.

# "MR X" "ARRIVES"

A familikeels-looking evil triangle-shaped figure stomped into X BURGER and looked around.

'It's Mr X!' shrieked Jamjar.

Dr Smell stood up and did a zombie-like salute in the direction of Mr X. 'On behalf of all your loyal customers, it is an honour to finally meet you, Master X!' he warbled.

'Yes, Master X,' said Splorg, standing up and zombie-saluting too. 'What can I do for you today? Clean your earholes out? Or perhaps I could brush your teeth with my toothbrush?'

'NOT!' screeched Not Bird, flying through the cloud of Nom Noms and swallowing five in one go.

# 'WHAT IN THE NAME OF X BURGER IS GOING ON HERE, WHEELIE?'

boomed Mr X.

Wheelie was standing in the middle of the restaurant, his arms waggling. 'GOOD AFTERNOON, MASTER,' he bleeped, his bad breath billowing into the air. 'JUST TAKING CARE OF A FEW, SHALL WE SAY, "CHALLENGING CUSTOMERS".'

Twoface pulled the trigger on his ray
gun and a stream of Hedgehog Cola
shot out the end of it, splurting
all over a light blue Nom Nom
that was zooming towards
his two faces.

'NOM NOM?' yelped the Nom Nom,
dropping to the floor like the opposite
of a hover-poo and turning to dust.

Mr X peered down at the pile of light
blue dust and scratched his head.
'WHAT IS THIS POWDERY SUBSTANCE?'
he said, and I remembered how dust
doesn't exist in the future.

'Twoface, it works! The Hedgehog Cola really works!' cried Jamjar, and I jumped in the air to give her a high five.

'NOM NOM!' growled a turquoise Nom Nom, a bit like Jamjar's Triangulator except hairier and more rectangular. It darted towards my nose and landed on the full-stop blob on the end of it.

'WAAAHHH!!! Not my full-stop nose blob!' I cried as Twoface pointed his pistol at my nose and pulled the trigger.

'BLEURGH!' I shouted as Hedgehog Cola splurted into my face.

The turquoise Nom Nom fell to the floor and exploded into a billion tiny pieces. 'Only another seven hundred and eighty twelve billion zillion left!' said Twoface, aiming at another one.

'Forget about the Nom Noms, Twoface!' I cried. 'Once we've destroyed the Nom Nom Queen they'll all be goners!'

'Oh yeah!' said Twoface, and we both turned round to face Wheelie. 'Let's see how old Queenie likes Hedgehog Cola!' Twoface grinned.

# "THE
"NOM
"NOM
"QUEEN

Mr X pulled a set of keys out of his pocket and pressed a tiny button on one of them. His giant metal scorpion bleeped, the way my mum and dad's car does when they unlock it, and he headed back out of X BURGER and jumped into its cockpit.

'THINK YOU CAN SCUPPER MY PLANS DO YOU, RATBOY?' he boomed, flicking a switch, and the scorpion's eyes blinked red. Its tail whipped into the shape of a question mark and a bright green laser, exackeely like the one that zapped my bin when Mr X stole it, shot out the end of it and through the door into the restaurant.

'Twoface, watch out!' cried Jamjar as the laser zipped past his ray gun, missing it by a billimetre.

'Now, Twoface!' I shouted, pointing towards Wheelie. 'Shoot the Nom Nom Queen now!'

Mr X's scorpion stepped forwards, its tail taking aim at Twoface's ray gun. 'OPERATION KEELNESS TIMES A MILLIKEELS!' shouted Twoface, pulling the trigger.

A bright green laser shot from the scorpion's tail, hitting Twoface's ray gun at the exact millisecond a stream of Hedgehog Cola squirted out of the end of it.

'WAAAHHH!!! My ray gun!' cried Twoface as it flew into the air and glowed green, then disappeared.

'THAT'LL TEACH YOU TO MESS WITH MR X!' boomed Mr X, as the stream of Hedgehog Cola splurted straight into Wheelie.

The ground started to rumble and the windows shook.

'X SERVANTS, DESTROY THESE INVADERS!' boomed Mr X, and Dr Smell, the hover-cap man, the old lady in the hover-wheelchair and Splorg started marching towards us, their arms stretched out in front of them like actual real-life zombies.

'BUUURRRPPPP!!!' croaked a noise from inside Wheelie's belly, and I dived under a table, pulling Twoface and Jamjar with me.

Wheelie's lid flipped shut, then opened wide again. 'I DO APOLOGISE, SIR. MUST'VE BEEN SOMETHING I ATE,' he bleeped, as the Nom Nom Queen splurged out of his belly into mid air and exploded into a billikeels stinking pieces.

# "NO MORE" "NOM NOMS"

Seven hundred and eighty twelve billion zillion Nom Noms stopped dead in their tracks, twitched their noses, then burst into smitherkeels.

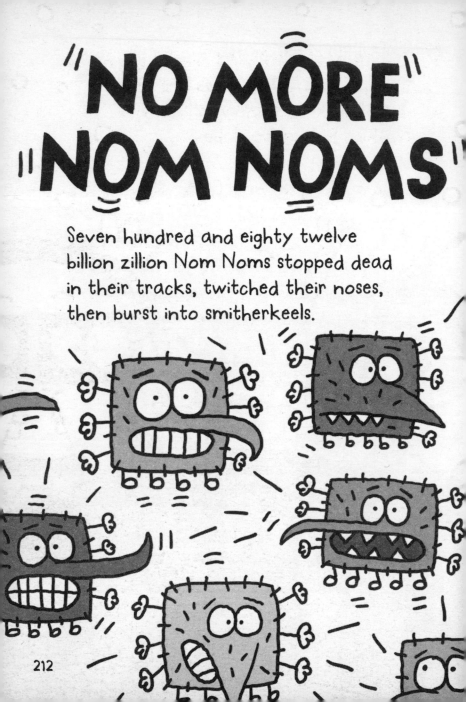

'YIPPEE-KEEL-KAYAY!' I cried, hugging Jamjar and Twoface as Nom Nom dust fell like the snow in Harry No-hands's plastic globe.

Wheelie was lying on his side, his lid flapping in my direction. 'RATBOY... IS THAT YOU?' he bleeped, and Jamjar pointed her Triangulator at him.

'The explosion must've reset his wiring!' she smiled.

Mr X glared through the window of X BURGER from inside his scorpion and wailed. He pulled a lever on his dashboard and the scorpion reared up on its back legs. Its tail sniffed the air, stopping dead when its laser-hole spied our table.

Splorg and the other zombie-customers had stopped marching and were blinking slowly, rubbing the ends of their noses like they'd woken up from a very big bad dream.

'Is it just me or can you taste cardboard?' said Dr Smell, and the hover-cap man nodded.

Mr X hovered his finger above a big scary-looking button. 'AND NOW YOU WILL ALL **BE** CARDBOARD!' he boomed.

'Eh? What does that mean?' said Twoface.

'It means get the keelness out of here!' I cried, forward-rolling over to Wheelie and pulling him towards the door by the handle.

'NOT!' screeched Not Bird as the floor started to shake.

Jamjar held on to the Floaty Note 6000 and grabbed Twoface's and Splorg's hands. 'GIDDY UP, FLOATY!' she screamed, floating after me.

# COME BACK WHEELIE!

'IT'S GREEN ZAPPY LASER TIME!'
cackled Mr X as we tumbled on
to the pavement outside X BURGER.

'RELEASE ME THIS INSTANT!' bleeped
Wheelie, wriggling free from my grip
and pulling himself up one of Mr X's
giant metal scorpion's legs with his
yellow washing up gloves.

'Wheelie, come back!' I cried, and
I looked over at Jamjar. 'I thought
you said the explosion had reset his
wiring!'

'It must've been a temporary blip,' said
Jamjar. 'Leave him Ratboy, let's GO!'
she shouted, running off down
Tinderbox Alley with Twoface and
Splorg in the direction of Bunny Deli.

'But I can't!' I wailed. 'Wheelie's my
only hope for getting home!'

Wheelie had reached the scorpion's cockpit and was banging one of his fists on its window. 'LET ME IN, MASTER X!' he bleeped.

'THERE'S A GOOD WHEELIE!' smiled Mr X, taking his finger off the scary-looking button and pressing a less scary-looking one. The cockpit window whooshed open and Wheelie flapped his lid.

'BUUUURRRRRPPPPP!!!!' he burped, straight into Mr X's face.

'GAAAAHHHH!!!!' screamed Mr X as a cloud of bin breath seeped into the scorpion's cockpit. 'MY CONTROL PANEL! THE BIN BREATH IS MELTING ITS CIRCUIT BOARDS!' he boomed.

Wheelie slid back down the scorpion's leg and wheeled up to me. 'ANYTHING ELSE I CAN DO FOR YOU TODAY, MR RATBOY, SIR?' he bleeped.

'Wheelie, you're the keelest!' I cried, giving him a hug.

Mr X turned round in his scorpion and scuttled off down the street. 'THIS ISN'T THE LAST YOU'VE SEEN OF ME, RATBOY!' he cackled, disappearing round the corner.

# BACK IN BUNNY DELI

Me, Wheelie and Not Bird caught up with Jamjar, Twoface, Splorg and Floaty, and we all strolled back to Bunny Deli as a storm cloud floated in front of the two suns.

'What in the unkeelness have you lot been up to? And what IS that powdery stuff?' said Bunny when we walked in half an hour later, all of us covered in Nom Nom dust.

'Oh not much,' said Splorg, sitting down at our table and peering at Malcolm the Smellnu. 'Cor, I could murder a cheesebleurgher!' he grinned, and a Cheesebleurgher Meal Deal fizzled to life in front of his nostrils.

He bit into his burger and looked up. 'Sorry about that zombie stuff by the way . . .' he said, and Wheelie flapped his lid.

'ME TOO, CHAPS. I DON'T KNOW WHAT CAME OVER ME,' he bleeped, and I Future-Ratboy-chuckled to myself, imagining what my mum, dad and little sister would think when I turned up back home with a talking bin.

'That's OK,' said Jamjar, putting two of her arms round them both. 'It's just good to have you back!'

Dennis, the official Bunny Deli bin, floated over and sniffed Wheelie's bum like a dog.

'HEE HEE, HELLO LITTLE FELLOW!' said Wheelie, patting him on the lid as the door to Bunny Deli whooshed open.

Dr Smell tiptoed in all sheepishly. He was followed by the hover-cap man and the old lady in the hover-wheelchair. 'Only us!' smiled Dr Smell. 'Not too late for a cheesebleurger is it, Bunny?'

'NOT!' squawked Not Bird, and Bunny grinned, which made us all smile too.

'Come in, come in!' she said, and she sat them down at a table together, which was awkward for them, seeing as they didn't actukeely know each other that well.

Twoface nicked one of Splorg's zigzaggedy chips and slotted it into his mouth. 'Spose you'll be off home soon then, Ratboy,' he said. 'All you need now is some lightning . . .'

I peered over at Wheelie. 'What d'you reckon?' I said, glancing through the window. 'Looks like there's a storm coming!'

Wheelie scratched his lid. 'ABOUT THAT, SIR,' he said. 'THERE'S AN AWFUL LOT OF NOM NOM DUST TO CLEAR UP, AND I DO SO HATE TO LEAVE A MESS.'
He looked down at Dennis. 'PLUS I'VE NEVER REALLY HAD A FRIEND BEFORE...'

Jamjar shuffled up to me and put one of her arms round my shoulders. 'You CAN'T go yet, Ratboy!' she said. 'We'll miss you too much!'

'I'll miss you lot too,' I said.

'Plus there's Mr X to take care of!' said Twoface, and I remembered Mr X scuttling off in his scorpion, saying how he had something in store for us.

'But we went to all that trouble to get Wheelie back!' I said, and I thought of my mum and dad and little sister sitting on the sofa at home, wondering if I was OK.

The street outside lit up, and thunder boomed in the distance.

'Pleeeease stay for a bit longer, Future Ratboy!' said Splorg. 'There'll always be another storm!'

I glanced over at Wheelie, who was stroking Dennis on the lid, and sighed. 'Well, there do seem to be a LOT of storms here in the future,' I said. 'And I spose it doesn't really matter if I stay a FEW more days - as long as I zap myself back to the exact billisecond I left . . .'

# JAMJAR HELD HER BREATH.

'Oh go on then - just until we've got rid of Mr X!' I said, and me, Splorg, Jamjar and Twoface all high-fived each other, which actukeely took quite a long time, what with all of Jamjar's hands.

'Ooh, I know what I was gonna say!' said Bunny, once all the high fives were finished. 'Did you get those bits I asked for?'

Jamjar plonked her carrier bag down on the table and pulled out the hand cream, the nail varnish and the soap. 'TA DA!' she smiled and Bunny picked them all up with three of her hands.

'Oh no, this won't do at all,' she said, peering at the little bottle of nail varnish and shaking her head. 'Electric Blue? I wanted Hot Pink! And this hand cream is the small tube. What have I got, five hands?' she laughed, holding up all ten.

The Floaty Note 6000 curled its top over, trying to read its scribbly writing. 'Erm . . .' it chirped, looking up at Jamjar.

'You don't mind popping out again do you, gang?' said Bunny.

Twoface groaned and Splorg rolled his black eyeballs. Jamjar's glasses slid down her nose.

I pushed Jamjar's glasses back up her nose and scraped out of my chair. 'Not at all!' I chuckled, wandering over to the door with Jamjar, Twoface, Splorg, Not Bird and Wheelie. Oh yeah, and Floaty and Dennis too.

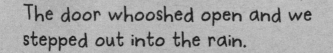

The door whooshed open and we stepped out into the rain.

'Won't be long, Bunny!' said Twoface,
just as my telly belly did a crackle.
I peered down at the little screen and
spotted a familikeels-looking vending
machine being held up to the sky in the
claws of a giant metal scorpion.

'On second thoughts . . .' I said,
starting to run down Shnozville
High Street.

# "ABOUT THE" "AUTHOR"

Jim Smith is the keelest kids' book author in the whole world amen.

He graduated from art school with first class honours (the best you can get) and went on to create the branding for a sweet little chain of coffee shops.

He also designs cards and gifts under the name Waldo Pancake.

THINKING UP
NEXT BOOK

First published in Great Britain 2016
by Jelly Pie an imprint of Egmont UK Ltd
The Yellow Building, 1 Nicholas Road, London W11 4AN

Text and illustration copyright © Jim Smith 2016
The moral rights of the author-illustrator have been asserted.

ISBN 978 1 4052 6915 5

1 3 5 7 9 10 8 6 4 2

www.futureratboy.com
www.egmont.co.uk

A CIP catalogue record for this title is available from the
British Library

Printed and bound in Great Britain by the CPI Group

56630/1

MIX
Paper
FSC   FSC® C018306

# PRAISE FOR MY

# "OTHER" BOOKS

'Will make you
laugh out loud,
cringe and
snigger, all at
the same time'
-LoveReading4Kids

LOVE?'
-Sun

cheeky'
-Booktictac,
Guardian Online Review

**Waterstones
Children's
Book Prize
Shortlistee!**

'The review of the eight
year old boy in our house...
"Can I keep it to give to a friend?"
Best recommendation you
can get' - Observer

'I LAUGHED
SO MUCH, I
THOUGHT THAT
I WAS GOING
TO BURST!'
Finbar, aged 9

'HUGELY
ENJOYABLE,
SURREAL
CHAOS'
-Guardian

I am still not a Loser
The Roald Dahl
FUNNY
PRIZE
WINNER 2013